My Moon

by Sarah Jane Wyman

Illustrated by Roni King

This book is a work of fiction. The names, characters, places and incidents are products of the writer's imagination or have been used fictitiously and are not to be construed as real. Any resemblance to persons, living or dead, actual events, locale or organisations is entirely coincidental. All rights are reserved. No part of this book may be used or reproduced in any form by any electronic, mechanical, or any other device now known or invented hereafter without the permission of the author, except in the case of brief quotations embodied in critical articles and reviews. These forms include, but are not limited to xerography, photocopying, scanning, recording, distributing via internet means, information storage and retrieval systems. Because of the dynamic nature of the internet, any web address or links contained in this book may have changed since publication and may no longer be valid.

Copyright © 2024 Sarah Jane Wyman

ISBN: 978-1-962825-26-9

What lives in this book is a true story. It is the story of a little girl whose father shared with her the power of imagination in the most interstellar way. A small Massachusetts pantry became the launchpad for the most magnificent journey through the stars. It is my deepest hope in a society of social media and distraction that this book will re-ignite the lost magic and power that lies within a child's imagination.

My Moon is truly a labor of love, family and friends.

To my brother, Steve, you recognized the magic in the words and connected me with the inspirational illustrator, Roni King, who captured the essence of the story with delightful perfection. You also remember those moments years ago when we both journeyed to the moon together with Dad.

To my mom, Margie, you are my best friend and taught me that anything is possible if you believe, and I promise not to let you down and write more books.

To my angel friend, Shawna of SCR Creative and Consulting, you have backed the publishing of this book from day one knowing this story will touch many. You guided me as managing editor, publishing consultant, book event planner, social media and PR manager, and "mommy meeting" co-conspirator – often brainstorming over a glass of wine.

A heartfelt thanks to my fiancé, Matt, whose belief in me made this dream a reality. My deepest gratitude for your support and love.

To my children, Sophie and Sam, who leaned into a family and childhood dynamic that was challenging but full of love and loyalty. Being a mom is the most precious gift and the two of you are the true works of art in my life.

This book is especially dedicated to my father, Rudd. His passion and love for art, writing and creative power are cherished gifts he passed down to me. The beauty of this story is that I lived it and every day, I am reminded that we all have the power of imagination inside us. And if, just if, we open our hearts and set it free, anything is possible. Thanks for the endless trips to the moon, Dad.

I love you,

Sarah Jane

See it? There. Above the trees.

Some believe… is cheddar cheese.

A yellow, magic, ball of light,

Watching, as we sleep at night.

From here on Earth, so small it seems.

A wonderlight with radiant beams.

But hear this story, I will tell.

About a moon I know so well.

It started once upon a time,
And changed my life forever.
The coolness of that summer night,
Reflecting fireflies in flight.

The last dish dried and put away,
The darkness creeping in on day.
My father stood and winked at me.
A special wink, meant just for me.

And in one heartbeat, from my chair,
He swept me up into the air.
High on his shoulders, eyes closed tight,
We ventured out into the night.

In moonlight stillness of the air,
I squeezed his hand. Are you still there?
"Stay quiet... We will take off soon."
A secret journey to the Moon.

Behind my eyes, a something quivered.
Through my body, something shivered.
We lifted off, above the trees,
Escaping earthly boundaries.

"Don't be afraid..just hold on tight."
"We're flying! Gliding, through the night"
I closed my eyes, yet I could see,
My Moon was waiting just for me.

I felt the night clouds touch my face,
Together into outer space.
My backyard now a speck of sand,
A tiny Earth of sea and land.

Then suddenly, a door flew wide.
Fantasmagoric things inside.
A world of cosmic, lunar things,
Built of free imaginings.

We whizzed by stars, who smiled at me.

Past Venus, Mars, and Mercury.

A glittery web of spangled beams,

Reflecting prisms, fairy dreams.

A spaceship flew right by my ear.

"Hello THERE. Welcome to HERE."

I heard a small voice beckon me,

"Enjoy the view…The ride is free!"

Moonslides, twirling, swirling beams,
Blending colors from my dreams.
Night rainbows stretching way up high,
Painting laughter on my sky.

I squeeze the hand that holds me tight.
I wish my moon, with all my might.
And suddenly, my heart is free,
My Moon is smiling down on me.

My Moon is filled with dreams I make.

Its craters filled with chocolate cake.

Here I can do ANYTHING,

Here I am free, to just be ME!

A brilliant star, I'm shining bright.

Surrounded by the whitest light.

Radiating and creating,

Being ME, for ALL to see.

Now look at me, a Moonbeam tree!
My branches reaching, stretching free.
With leaves of gold, I don't grow old,
I watch the universe unfold.

A Princess of the Night and Light,

Yes, Royalty, My Moon and me.

We rule together, as we please,

Our magic kingdom made of cheese.

I think. A Moon Knight I could be.
Protecting all the galaxy.
Perched high upon my firefly,
Sheltering the midnight sky.

Or perhaps a Moon Bug, if you please.
My favorite food, of course, Swiss cheese.
Scouting out new Moon Bug houses,
Making friends with Moonbeam Mouses.

Then suddenly a moonthing quivered.
Deep in my heart, that moonthing shivered.
"Hold tight," a whisper in my ear.
"We must go back," the dawn is near.

And then a radiant arch of light.
A giant moonslide through the night.
Swept off my feet, I squeezed his hand,
Then with a BUMP, I felt the land.

My eyes now open. What do I see?

My backyard, just as it should be.

I looked up to the midnight sky.

A secret smile, My Moon and I.

And from our journey, this I know,

The Moon is not that far to go.

To any planet, any star,

To any country, near or far.

The magic is inside, you see,
It's inside you and inside me.
The wonder of imagination,
Your Moon is your own creation.

So close your eyes, as I close mine.
Your Moon is there, inside your mind.
The world is waiting. Yes, it's true.
So paint the dreams inside of you.

And me? I know that I was there.

Some folks may smirk, but I don't care.

I know, wherever I may be,

My Moon is shining down on me.

THE END

About the Author, Sarah Jane Wyman

Sarah so beautifully shares this deeply personal story from her childhood. Her story is an invitation to the reader to join her on a special journey to the moon exploring life's meaning of love, safety, and friendship. Sarah grew up in New England where creativity and artisanship are regularly celebrated. Her creative expression developed at Emerson College, where she studied communications and performing arts.

She resides in beautiful Portland, Maine and as a single mom, she relied heavily on artistic inspiration to create a childhood filled with magic. All children should feel loved, safe and experience the freedom to grow with the world as individuals. For Sarah, writing has always been an adventure and whether poetry or short stories, she expresses gratitude for the limitless freedom associated with putting words on paper. To have this book shared with children and to put it in the hands of her 96-year-old father, is nothing short of a dream come true.

About the Illustrator, Roni King

Roni is a self-taught artist especially in acrylics, watercolor and fiber art. She started her own business designing and sewing appliquéd children's bibs more than 30 years. Roni also created the painted designs for "Ornament of the Year" for the Church Fair for 40 years. She resides in a beautiful seaside town in Massachusetts where she continues to create magic through her artwork. She especially enjoyed illustrating for this book because of the very imaginative verses.

www.ingramcontent.com/pod-product-compliance
Lightning Source LLC
Chambersburg PA
CBHW041414010526
44107CB00016B/1160